A BEACH FOR ALBERT

by **Eleanor May** • Illustrated by **Deborah Melmon**

THE KANE PRESS / NEW YORK

For Bridget, who has her own pool, too!—E.M.

Acknowledgments: We wish to thank the following people for their helpful advice and review of the material contained in this book: Susan Longo, Early Childhood and Elementary School Teacher, Mamaroneck, NY; and Rebeka Eston Salemi, Kindergarten Teacher, Lincoln School, Lincoln, MA.

Special thanks to Susan Longo for providing the Fun Activities in the back of this book.

Library of Congress Cataloging-in-Publication Data

May, Eleanor.
A beach for Albert / by Eleanor May ; illustrated by Deborah Melmon.
pages cm. — (Mouse math)
"With fun activities!"
Summary: When the People go to the beach, Albert the mouse decides to make a beach of his own in the backyard sandbox, but first he must figure out how to fill a big bowl with water for swimming, using the concept of volume/capacity.
ISBN 978-1-57565-530-7 (library reinforced binding : alk. paper) — ISBN 978-1-57565-531-4 (pbk. : alk. paper) — ISBN 978-1-57565-532-1 (e-book)
[1. Mice—Fiction. 2. Beaches—Fiction. 3. Mathematics—Fiction.] I. Melmon, Deborah, illustrator.
II. Title.
PZ7.M4513Bef 2013
[E]—dc23   2012051087

1 3 5 7 9 10 8 6 4 2

First published in the United States of America in 2013 by Kane Press, Inc.
Printed in the United States of America
WOZ0713

Book Design: Edward Miller

Mouse Math is a registered trademark of Kane Press, Inc.

Visit us online at **www.kanepress.com**

 Like us on Facebook
facebook.com/kanepress

Follow us on Twitter
@KanePress

Dear Parent/Educator,

"I can't do math." Every child (or grownup!) who says these words has at some point along the way felt intimidated by math. For young children who are just being introduced to the subject, we wanted to create a world in which math was not simply numbers on a page, but a part of life—an adventure!

Enter Albert and Wanda, two little mice who live in the walls of a People House. Children will be swept along with this irrepressible duo and their merry band of friends as they tackle mouse-sized problems and dilemmas. (And sometimes *cat-sized* problems and dilemmas!)

Each book in the **MOUSE MATH**® series provides a fresh take on a basic math concept. The mice discover solutions as they, for instance, use position words while teaching a pet snail to do tricks or count the alarmingly large number of friends they've invited over on a rainy day—and, lo and behold, they are doing math!

Math educators who specialize in early childhood learning used their expertise to make sure each title would be as helpful as possible to young kids—and to their parents and teachers. Fun activities at the end of the books and on our website encourage children to think and talk about math in ways that will make each concept clear and memorable.

As with our award-winning Math Matters® series, our aim is to captivate children's imaginations by drawing them into the story, and so into the math at the heart of each adventure. It is our hope that kids will want to hear and read the **MOUSE MATH** stories again and again and that, as they grow up, they will approach math with enthusiasm and see it as an invaluable tool for navigating the world they live in.

Sincerely,

Joanne Kane

Joanne E. Kane
Publisher

The People were heading off to the beach.

"I wish we could go to the beach, too," Albert said. "Swimming, sand, and sun!"

"It's sunny here," his sister, Wanda, said.
"And we can play in the big sandbox while the
People are away."

Albert and Wanda climbed into the sandbox.

"I have an idea!" Albert said.
"What if we fill this giant bowl with water?
Then we'll have sand *and* swimming, like a
real beach."

"That's a big bowl," Wanda said.
"I'll bet it holds a lot of water."

Albert smiled. "I know! Isn't it great?
All our friends can come swimming, too!"

"How do you plan to fill it up?" Wanda asked.

Albert held up his plastic pail.
"Watch me!" he said.

8

Albert ran to the spigot by the
People House.
He turned on the water and
filled his pail.

Then he ran back and dumped
the water out into the bowl.

Quickly, Albert scurried back and forth . . .

then not quite so quickly . . .

then not quickly at all.

Albert stared down into the bowl.
"It isn't very full," he said.

"Albert," Wanda said, "suppose you had
a whole bunch of those plastic pails.
How many would it take to fill the bowl?"

"A lot!" Albert said.

Wanda said, "Well, that's how many pails of water it will take to fill the bowl. A LOT!
And every pail of water means another trip for you."

Albert looked at Wanda's pail.

"I have an idea!" he said. "Let's trade pails. Your pail is bigger than mine. If I use a bigger pail, I won't have to make as many trips."

"My pail is taller," Wanda said. "But yours is wider. They hold the same amount of water—see?"

She poured the water from Albert's pail into her own.

"Oh!" Albert said. "You're right!"

Albert scampered over to a doll teacup.
"This cup is taller *and* wider," he said.
"I'll bet it holds twice as much as our pails!"

He took the cup and
filled it at the spigot.

The cup did hold twice as much water.
It was twice as heavy, too.
Wanda peered over the edge of the sandbox.
"Albert, do you need help?"

"I—can—do—it—" Albert wheezed.
"I'm—almost—
Hey! Look at that!"

THUD. Albert landed on the ground.

"Oh, Albert," Wanda said. "Are you okay?"

Albert sat up smiling.
"I have an idea!"

"See that toy dump truck?" he said. "It's perfect!
I can put a LOT of water in the back. Then I'll drive
the truck right up to the bowl and dump it in!
In just a few trips, the bowl will be full!"

"Albert, do you know *how* to drive a toy truck?"
Wanda asked.

"Sure!" Albert said. "I saw the People playing with it.
The green button makes it go forward like this—"

Wanda leaped out of the way.

"—and the red button makes it stop."

Albert pulled the truck up to the spigot.
He climbed up and turned on the water.
"See?" he said. "Easy-cheesy!"

Albert started the truck again.
"Now, *this* button makes it turn . . . *WHOA!*"

Wanda chased after him.
"Albert, make it stop going in circles!"

"I can't!" Albert cried. "The button's stuck!"

Albert pushed all the buttons he could reach.
The dump truck stopped.
The back part tipped.

Albert looked down at Wanda.
She was very wet.

"Oops," Albert said. "I guess that
was the 'dump' button I pushed."

"I guess it was," Wanda said.

"I'm sorry, Wanda," Albert said. "But I have an idea—"

"No!" Wanda cut him off. "*I* have an idea."
She turned and squelched away.

Albert sat on the edge of
the sandbox, chin in paw.

Then Wanda came back.
Behind her came Albert's best friend, Leo.
Behind Leo came his sister, Lucy.
Behind Lucy came all their other friends—
and every one of them was carrying a pail.

Albert and Wanda watched all their helpers at work.
"Wow!" Albert said. "The bowl is filling up fast now!"

"I'm sorry the dump truck didn't work out," Wanda said.

Albert grinned. "Actually, I have an idea. . . ."

Once the mice had filled the bowl with water,
Albert filled the truck with mice.
"Ready?" he yelled, and pushed a button.
The mice slid straight into the water.

"Now the bowl is full of water AND mice," Wanda said.

"Not QUITE full," Albert pointed out.

And they jumped in!

A Beach for Albert supports children's understanding of **capacity**, an important topic in early math learning. Use the activities below to extend the math topic and to reinforce children's early reading skills.

ENGAGE

Remind children that the cover of a book can tell them a lot about the story inside.

▶ Before reading the story, invite children to look at the cover illustration as you read the title aloud. Ask: *What do you think this story is about? What is Albert doing? Why do you think he's doing this?* You may wish to record children's responses and refer back to them at the end of the story.

▶ Talk about the word *capacity* and what it means. (In this story, *capacity* refers to the amount of liquid a container can hold.) Help children understand *capacity* by gathering containers of various sizes and shapes. Ask questions such as: *Which of these containers do you think holds the most water? Why? How could you prove your answer?*

▶ Tell children that Albert runs into a big problem in this story! Ask: *What do you think the problem is?* Say: *Let's read the story and find out!*

LOOK BACK

▶ After reading the story, ask children if they correctly guessed Albert's problem. Discuss the ways in which he and Wanda tried to solve the problem of how to fill the bowl. Ask: *Did all of Albert's ideas work? Why or why not? At the end of the story, how did the mice manage to fill the bowl so quickly?*

▶ Revisit the meaning of *capacity*. Have children look at the illustrations and find all the containers the mice used to fill the bowl. Encourage children to talk about each container in terms of its capacity. (You may want to start a list of containers to help children make the connection.)

☙ TRY THIS!

Have children work in pairs or small groups. For each group you will need:
- a supply of water and a towel in case of spills!
- a container (containers should all be the same size; e.g. coffee tins)
- a variety of different-sized cups or jars (you may wish to use 1 cup, ½ cup, ⅓ cup, and ¼ cup measuring cups)

▷ Explain to children that their task is to fill their container with water as quickly and carefully as possible. Encourage them first to think about which cup they should use.

▷ Make note of which group fills their container to the top first. Ask that group to describe how they did it so quickly. Encourage them to use the word *capacity*.

▷ Empty the containers. Now have each group use a specific cup to refill their container. (For example, group A might use the largest cup, group B a smaller cup, etc.) Ask a volunteer from each group to record the number of cups it takes to fill their container.

▷ After all the containers are full, make a list of the group results. Direct children's attention to the list and ask: *Which group used the greatest number of cups to fill their container? Which group used the least number of cups? Why do you think this is?*

Bonus: Explain that *capacity* can also refer to the amount of dry materials a container can hold. Dry out the containers, and repeat the activity using rice, sand, or beans. Ask: *Did the material used make a difference in the number of cups needed to fill the container?*

☙ THINK!

For each pair or group of children you will need: a small box such as a shoebox (same size for each group), standard-sized cubes or blocks, and a recording sheet with two columns—one labeled "Prediction" (or "Guess") and one labeled "Actual Number."

▷ Tell children they are going to make a block building.

▷ Give each group a box and cubes. Ask: *How many cubes do you think it will take to fill the shoebox?* Record their predictions. Then record their actual findings. Discuss the results. Encourage children to use the word *capacity*.

◆ FOR MORE ACTIVITIES ◆

visit www.kanepress.com/mousemath-activities.html